Stormy Weather

Debi Gliori

BLOOMSBURY

LONDON BERLIN NEW YORK

Pull up the quilt, turn out the light,
dear child, it's time to say goodnight.
In darkness black and soft and deep,
I'll watch beside you while you sleep.

Across the world
in many beds
a million goodnight
stories read

of frogs and kings
and gingerbread,
then lights go out,
goodnights are said.

Then should the oceans roar and rise and dark clouds race across the skies

I'd hold you tight and close and warm
and keep you safe all through the storm.

If thunder tore the night in two
and lightning played at peek~a~BOO

we'd watch the storm pass overhead,
then curl up safe and snug in bed.

And if that breeze became a gale ~
whipped leaves, snapped twigs, made branches flail

I'd wrap you safely in my wings and tell you tales of sleepy things.

And if it rained ten thousand rains
and torrents swept down streets to drains

we'd build a boat and sail away
to where the sun shines bright all day.

And if the snow began to fall,

flake on flake piled up miles tall

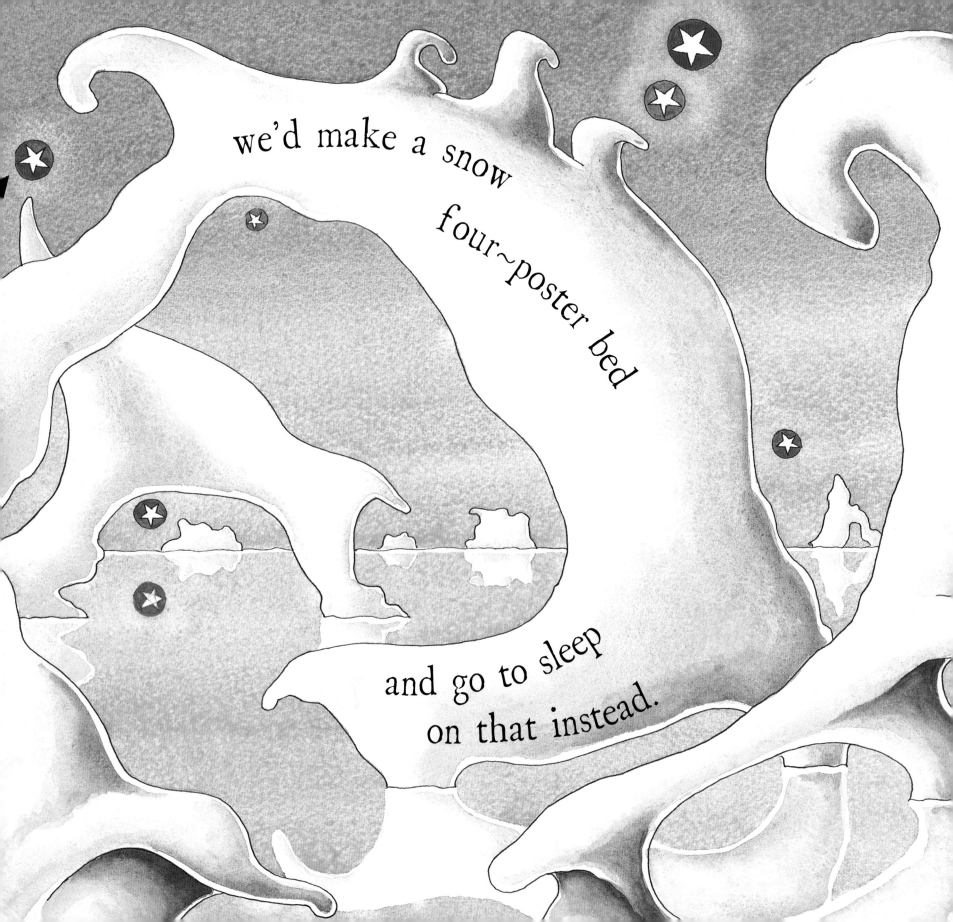

From North to South and East to West,
from cave to berg and twig to nest
a sleepy hush across the world,
small creatures in their beds are curled.

Sweet dreams beneath our sheltering sky,
the tides and winds our lullaby,

the stars our light, the whole night through
shine down so bright on me and you.